Mama Said, What?

———— ∞ ————

JULIA BUCHANAN

ISBN 978-1-68570-081-2 (paperback)
ISBN 978-1-68570-082-9 (digital)

Copyright © 2022 by Julia Buchanan

All rights reserved. No part of this publication may be reproduced, distributed, or transmitted in any form or by any means, including photocopying, recording, or other electronic or mechanical methods without the prior written permission of the publisher. For permission requests, solicit the publisher via the address below.

Christian Faith Publishing
832 Park Avenue
Meadville, PA 16335
www.christianfaithpublishing.com

Printed in the United States of America

To first and foremost my Lord and Savior Jesus Christ.
"For I know the plans I have for you," declares the Lord, "plans to prosper you and not to harm you, plans to give you hope and a future" (Jeremiah 29:11 NIV).

Acknowledgments

To my awesome husband of over fifty-two years, Richard L. Buchanan, thank you! From reading the earlier drafts to giving me advice and quotes and helping me make this book a reality. To Eric Michael Buchanan, thanks for pushing me into believing, "I can do this!" But I couldn't have done this without my sister, Pastor, Dr. Lola C. Hampton. Thank you for walking alongside me all the way. Every family should have a sister like Lola! She's always there for me, and without her, this book would not be in existence. A shout out to all my family!

Chapter 1

MY MAMA

Mama! Nannie Beatrice Porter was a widower at forty-two years old. Dad died in your arms on January 11, 1954. Leaving you to raise eight girls and one boy alone. I was only three when he died and can still picture us little ones looking over the guard rail on the stairs in our townhouse as the fire engine pulled up and the firemen wearing their big black-and-yellow uniforms, and succinctly came and took him out of your arms and put him on the stretcher. I was too young to know exactly what was happening then, but I felt something. Something just wasn't right. A few days later, we were ushered into this bright-lit room, looking at dad in his coffin. It was then that I wouldn't ever see my dad again. Oh, mama, today I can only imagine what was going through your mind. You never held a job. But because hindsight is twenty-twenty, I can now fill in the blanks of those years following his death.

The old black-and-white snapshots/pictures of you out having fun with your friends showed me just how alive and how beautiful you were. I know that you did date and even got close to a few men but never remarried because you said, "You didn't want men to be hanging around your girls." The sacrifice you gave, for our protection, was beyond amazing because most moms would have jumped at the chance to get some help. You hung in there. With your belief in Christ, scripture became alive for you. "I can do all things through

Christ who strengthens me" (Philippians 4:13). In retrospect, that sacrifice reminds me of another who gave up his life for me too, Jesus Christ! So thank you, Mom. You didn't have to do that for us, but you did.

So if you're reading this from heaven, I want you to know that you did a wonderful, amazing, and extraordinary job raising us. You birthed in us to live a good, godly life. You took what life handed you, Mama, and you raised nine wonderful, independent, trustworthy, dedicated, and loving children.

Many reading this will wonder how in the world did you raise that many children especially alone? So let me quote you here: "When life hands you lemons, make lemonade." Or I'll quote my brother, McDowell Jr, who'd just reminded me of what you said about that very question: "It's not hard raising children. All you need are beans on the table, rags on their backs, and a shack for them to live in. And that's how I loved and raised my children!"

You sent us off to Peter's Rock Baptist Church every Sunday morning in Gary, Indiana, where we sang in the choir, went to Sunday School, and became lovers of God and His Son, Jesus Christ, as we listened to the preacher's sermons. How I remember the cute little dresses we wore to church because pants were made for boys. As a matter of fact, I don't think I ever wore pants to church until around 2015.

I can still see you in your housedress, sitting on the sofa with the Bible in your lap, reading it every day. I kept your last Bible because it was a part of you. Though worn and falling apart, my heart would ache as I held your Bible in my hands. I loved seeing your handwritten notes inside it. It just reminded me that you were here, alive, breathing! I miss your face and your warm tender embrace; your voice; your laughter and smile; and your quotes, teachings, wisdom, and love. You have left a legacy that's impacted not only me and my siblings but also for the generations that have followed—your grandchildren, great-, and great-great-grandchildren. We have taken in all that you gave us and embedded that legacy into your thirty-one grandchildren to appreciate life and family! Thanks, Mama!

Chapter 2

QUOTES, WHAT?

Now let's fast forward seventy years to today. Why a book now? Well, this book started out because of a complete misunderstanding. My sister called to tell me that she was writing her second book. She'd asked me and my husband to share some quotes we'd heard while growing up. I thought of many, and I set out to write them down.

One day, while my husband was talking on the phone with his brother, I decided to ask his brother if he remembered any quotes he had heard while growing up. He had said that he and his friends were just talking about "somebody ought to write a book of all the quotes we heard while growing up!" So off we were.

In the span of about two days, we had combined and collected over twenty-five of them. We were laughing so hard as we strolled through memory lane, reminiscing about those quotes. They'd brought back so many wonderful memories! It felt refreshing. Aww, the good ole days! Those were the days of playing in streets, petticoats, ponytails, penny candy, bobby socks, rotary phones, phone numbers you could remember. How we danced to songs like "The Roach," "The Twist," and so much more.

Chapter 3

CHRISTIAN QUOTES, WHAT?

Excited to have so many quotes to share, I started shooting them off to my sister. After sending her about ten or so via text, I'd soon realized she wasn't responding. Maybe she was busy, or at the gym, or preparing her sermon for that Sunday? So I decided to stop texting her and just call her. She answered right away, but I detected something was wrong when I heard her voice. In her response, she told me that she was getting the quotes but stopped reading them after she'd only read a couple of them. She lowered the hammer next by saying that she only wanted *Christian* quotes. Aww, man, I was downtrodden. I was so off course. From that moment on, I stopped texting them to her. But it set me off on another course—I had all these quotes and didn't want them all to go to waste, so I decided, "Why not just put them all into a book like my brother-in-law said?"

But now the realization hits. What would you name a book that is made up of so many life quotes that also envelopes the spirit of the past? That's when I thought of my own mom who'd raised nine children and my mother-in-law, Teresa Traylor, who raised ten. So in remembrance of these two awesome mothers who'd instilled so much wisdom into their children that I decided to call this book *Mama Said, What?* Not a *what* like "What?" but "What?"

Chapter 4

LIFE QUOTES, WHAT?

Life quotes are like precious gems. Once you have one, you never want to let it go. They're passed down from generation to generation. As I accumulated more and more of these precious gems, I was surprised to find out just how many quotes are out there. You'll find many quotes my mama said while growing up, like the *lemonade* one found in chapter 1 and also, "Rest your heart, child. Rest your heart." Between the quotes we'd accumulated in the beginning to the end, the book started taking root. I'd keep sticky notes around the house to make sure I'd capture any life quotes I'd hear from general conversations. Some are taken from the television or even stumbling on across the Internet.

So here we are.

Sidebar: Most of these quotes were gathered over the generations. The *baby boomers*, which is a term used to describe a person who was born between 1946 and 1964, heard and remembered many of these quotes. They helped shape us into the people we are today and should not be buried in the past and/or taken to the grave but should stay around for years to come.

The quotes reflect how times were back during the years growing up. We had such a different upbringing than the young people today. So with that in mind, I hope these quotes (our precious gems) bring a smile to your face as you go down memory lane. I hope young and old alike will share and enjoy them with your children and your grandchildren for many generations to come.

Chapter 5

THE WAY WE WERE, WHAT?

Gladys Knight said it best when she sang "The Way We Were/ Try to Remember" in 1974. Pay attention to some of the lyrics:

> Hey you know everybody is talkin' about the good old days, right. Well, let's talk about the good old days. Come to think of it, as bad as we think they are, these will become the good old days for our children. Try to remember that kind of September, when life was slow and oh so mellow. Try to remember and if you remember follow. Oh, why does it seem the past is always better. We look back and think, the winters were warmer, the grass was greener the skies were bluer, and smiles were bright.

She and the Pips nailed that song. They sang totally from the heart because the words written were true. I'm sure that those over sixty-five years old can agree with me on that.

Chapter 6

OUR MUSIC, WHAT?

Oh, how the music moved us. Our church music pierced and helped save our souls. Religious artists sang songs like "Precious Lord, Take My Hand" or Mahalia Jackson's song "Lord Don't Move the Mountain." What about "The Mighty Clouds of Joy?" "Two Wings?" Or Professor Johnson's "Give Me that Old Time Religion," Blind Willie Johnson's "The Lord Will Make a Way Somehow," and Rev. Robert Ballinger's "How I Got Over." These gospel artists are just a few who laid a firm foundation for our gospel music line.

Some of our R&B artists are Jimi Hendrix, Michael Jackson, Ray Charles, Ben E. King, Prince, Diana Ross, Ella Fitzgerald, Johnny Mathis, Ornette Coleman, Dionne Warwick, Whitney Houston, Nat King Cole, Phil Collins, Teddy Pendergrass and my all-time favorite Gladys Knight and the Pips singing "I Feel a Song (In My Heart)." (I cry every time I listen to it.)

I found this on the Internet:

> The 13 Popular Songs from the '50s and '60s that Were Actually Censored
>
> 1. "Splish Splash" by Bobby Darrin, 1958
> 2. "Wake Up Little Susie" by The Everly Brothers, 1957

3. "Puff, the Magic Dragon" by Peter, Paul and Mary, 1962
4. "Let's Spend the Night Together" by The Rolling Stones, 1967
5. "Brown Eyed Girl" by Van Morrison, 1967–
6. "Will You Still Love Me Tomorrow" by The Shirelles, 1960
7. "My Generation" by The Who, 1965
8. "God Only Knows" by The Beach Boys, 1966
9. "Louie, Louie" by The Kingsman, 1963
10. "Great Balls of Fire" by Jerry Lee Lewis, 1957
11. "Love Me Two Times" by The Doors, 1967
12. "Leader of the Pack" by The Shangri Las, 1965
13. "I Saw Mommy Kissing Santa Claus" by Jimmy Boyd, 1952

Here's what the History Channel says about music in the '50s:

Elvis Presley. Sam Cooke. Chuck Berry. Fats Domino. Buddy Holly. The 1950s saw the emergence of Rock 'n' Roll, and the new sound swept the nation. It helped inspire rockabilly music from Jerry Lee Lewis and Johnny Cash. People swayed to The Platters and The Drifters. Music marketing, changed, too: For the first time, music began to target youth.

CHAPTER 7

TEN COMMANDMENTS AND PRAYER, WHAT?

Mama made sure we were in church every Sunday. This was where all our religious foundations developed to make us better people. We grew in God's word. Learning and keeping the Ten Commandments kept us out of a lot of trouble. We learned that God heard and answered our prayers, especially learning something new in school or getting ready for that test. Reading the Bible taught us about God's love and His plans for us. And when the Ten Commandments and prayer were removed from the schools in 1962, all hell seemed to have broken loose. The baby boomers saw this effect right away.

Look at some of the problems developed since then:

1940	1990
1. Talking out of turn	1. Drug abuse
2. Chewing gum	2. Alcohol abuse
3. Making noise	3. Pregnancy
4. Running in the halls	4. Suicide
5. Cutting in line	5. Rape
6. Dress code violations	6. Robbery
7. Littering	7. Assault

MAMA SAID, WHAT?

Here's what David Barton of Wall Builders says:

> We have gone from public schools which taught moral principles and good citizenship with high scholastic achievement, to schools that have disrespect for authority, sex, drugs, anger, knives, guns, murder, no moral teachings, no mention of God and low SAT scores.

Every family had a family Bible.

A family Bible is a Bible handed down through a Christian family, with each successive generation, recording information about the family's history inside of it. Typically, this information consists of births, deaths, baptisms, confirmations, and marriages; family Bibles contain a "family record" or "family registry" section to record this information. People sometimes may place other items, such as holy cards, certificates, letters, newspaper cuttings, or hair clippings and photographs inside a family Bible. In the United Kingdom, they are found today and were especially common in the Victorian period, and are also found in the United States, Australia, and New Zealand. Family Bibles are often placed on a family's home altar, being regularly used for family prayer. They are often used as sources for genealogical research.

CHAPTER 8

THE GOLDEN RULE, WHAT?

Most of us did not have the benefit of sugarcoated lives growing up. Our parents loved us, true, but they meant business! No, meant, No! Not a "Go and sit in the corner and stay there until you apologize, no." It was more like, "Go, find my belt, or get me a switch, no!"

Many would agree that the Golden Rule is, "Do unto others as you would have them do unto you." True. But my mom or maybe your parents followed this golden rule, "Spare the rod, spoil the child!" Children weren't going to be their friends; they were parents!

I love this quote from Rev. Nancy Colier, LCSW:

> Assuming your role as the authority in your child's life is critical, and the more you assume that role, the more you will feel the wisdom of your own authority. Being the authority doesn't mean turning a deaf ear to your child's anger, disappointment, or anything else they feel. We can listen to our kids' emotions and thoughts while simultaneously holding our ground on what we know is best for them. Being the authority

in your kid's life doesn't mean being callous or insensitive, but it does mean being brave enough to stay strong in the face of a tsunami that might come back at you, knowing that your role is to be the grown up in the parent-child relationship, to be loving in your willingness to do what's best for your kids. Your role is not to be your child's friend.

Chapter 9

GANGS, WHAT?

We played in and on the streets and playgrounds until dusk without the fear of getting hurt or gunned down. It was a time of letting children be children. The only shooting by a gang then were your friends shooting marbles. You'll get your gang together to play baseball against the other kids on the other side of the neighborhood. Your gang loved playing hide-go-seek, riding your bike together, skating on steel skates that attached to your shoes, hopscotch, jumping rope, the Hula-Hoop, fun things that kept you outside until you heard your parent(s) call that it was time to come in. So safe. Our moms and dads knew where we were always.

Chapter 10

CHANNEL, WHAT?

Most of us grew up with one twelve-inch black-and-white television in our living room. Families mostly were large; remember contraceptive or birth control pills weren't available back then. And that twelve-inch TV only had four main channels: 2, 5, 7, and 9 with the VHF channels 26 and 32. TV sets came with an indoor antenna that most people called rabbit ears. Most of the time, you had to have someone take the rabbit ears and walk around the room and hold the antenna until you could get a decent picture. Or get a clothes hanger, or a fork hooked to the antennae to keep the picture on clearly. In the 1950s, there was no cable TV, no remote controls. Yes! You actually had to get up to turn the channel on or off the television sets.

CHAPTER 11

SOAPS, GAME SHOWS, AND SO MUCH MORE, WHAT?

During the weekdays when we were at school, and your dad was at work, our moms had access to the TV. They loved the soap operas *Search for Tomorrow, Guiding Light, All My Children, One Life to Live*, and *General Hospital* (they were the highlights for moms) or game shows like *What's My Line? Twenty-One*, or *Truth or Consequences*. Moms were home when we went to school and when we came home. They made sure we ate, and we ate whatever was before us. Or hear, "Kids in Africa are starving, and look at you, you better eat that food!" (Another quote, by the way.)

When our older siblings came home from school, their go-to show was Dick Clark's *American Bandstand*. Then finally after it ended, the younger siblings could finally watch The Three Stooges, *The Mickey Mouse* show, or *The Bozo Circus*.

Later we'd all gather around the TV to watch shows like the *Ed Sullivan Show, Amos 'n' Andy, Dragnet*, and *Wanted Dead or Alive*, but the best of all were *I Love Lucy, The Flintstones, Gilligan's Island, John Wayne*, and other westerns. Just all-around wholesome programs.

Here's a quote I discovered that mirrored my opinion:

I enjoyed watching westerns back then. It takes you back to a time when things were so easy, you always knew the good guy would prevail. Wish they would bring them back, but with TV censors, it would never last. Which is too bad. I'd watch that over reality shows!

Now there are thousands of TV channels to choose from. And it's sad that children today are exposed to more killing, sex, and hatred than ever before!

Here's a quote by Dave Taraldson:

> The "Golden Age of Hollywood" actually before the 1950s…way before the 1950s. The era declined rapidly with the advent of television. Before the '50s, movie theaters were the only game in town (except for live performances). Hollywood was a "magical" place with "magical" movie stars that entertained the masses. It had almost a religious following. People like Errol Flynn, W. C. Fields, Mae West, Laurel and Hardy, Charlie Chaplin, Fred Astaire and Ginger Rogers, etc., were bigger than life and were almost worshiped.
>
> When you could see movies "free" on a television screen, the movie theaters became less important and more people stayed home and watched. Then television started making higher quality programs and made-for-TV movies that made it less desirable to actually pay money to go see a movie at a theater. More and more stars made the transition to performing on television and the fascination with "superstars" gradually declined.
>
> The "Golden Age of Hollywood" doesn't refer to the quality of the movies, it refers to the reverence that the public had for the theaters and the movie stars.

CHAPTER 12

M, R, PG, PG13, AND G, WHAT?

As far back as I can remember, the clergy (pastors, the reverends) had seats on the TV boards to make sure that no sexy or violent shows aired on television. The clergy was there to protect what people heard and saw on television. It was just a known fact that we were assured by this group of clergy that no one would be shocked by inappropriate content programs.

Later, M, R, PG, PG13, and G ratings were commissioned in 1996 to give advance information on material in television programming that might be unsuitable for their children. Here's a quote from Dennis Mulgannon:

> Churches and religion were a lot more influential in the daily lives of people in the USA, dating back even before the 20th Century, which carried forth through to the late 1970s.

Even *Singin' in the Rain* and Jerry Lewis, Bob Hope, Sammy Davis Jr., and Bing Crosby movies like *Road to Bali*, *Lady and the Tramp*, and *To Catch a Thief* were screened before being released to the public.

Chapter 13

MOVIES, 46 CENTS, WHAT?

Mama would give us $1 to go to the movie theaters. The bus ride then was 10¢ to and 10¢ back for the bus ride. There was 46¢ for a movie and enough money left for popcorn or candy. Those were the days!

CHAPTER 14

MANUAL WASHING MACHINES, OUTHOUSES, WHAT?

"Cleanliness is next to godliness." Hey, that's one of the quotes below. Well, it is just that we had clean clothes. Clothes, sheets, and so forth were usually cleaned in "a basin filled with hot sudsy water and a washboard," or some were blessed to get the washing machines that had the manual wringers on them. Our clothes were dried on outdoor clotheslines.

Once we took a trip to Arkansas to visit our grandmother. It was a very rural town she lived in; dirt roads, lots of cotton fields, and there were outhouses. Mom, her sisters and brother, and generations before them picked cotton to make money. I remember having to go to the bathroom, and they told me where it was. I had to go outside? My brother reminded me just recently that toilet paper was a rare commodity back then. Remember, the old Sears Roebuck catalog? Just think of it as the Amazon of the day. Anything you needed, you just order from that catalog. And guess what those pages from the catalog were used for? Yep, toilet paper.

MAMA SAID, WHAT?

Here's an interesting document found on the Internet:

> In rural agrarian communities, handfuls of straw were frequently used, but one of the most popular items to use for clean-up was dried corncobs. They were plentiful and quite efficient at cleaning. They could be drawn in one direction or turned on an axis. They were also softer on tender areas than you might think. Even after toilet paper became available, some people in Western states still preferred corncobs when using the outhouse.

Chapter 15

PENNY CANDY, WHAT?

The corner store sold penny candy, which was yep, "penny candy"! For the most part, the days of penny candy are long gone. Although I'm sure you may occasionally find a small store or a specialty store or gumball machine that will still give you a small piece of candy for only a penny, I haven't been to one yet. Many stores have increased their prices quite a bit since the days of penny candy.

A few examples of candy in those days are Good & Plenty, Life Savers, Jawbreakers, or candy cigarettes.

Chapter 16

TV, CELL PHONE, COMPUTER, AND VIDEO GAME BABYSITTERS, WHAT?

We had real talks around the dinner table, no distractions from the video games and cell phones of today. The first cell phone was invented in 1973, but it didn't become available to the public until 1983. Today, kids as early as one-year-old own one.

Back in our day, God forbid we asked for a bike, or even new shoes, and the like. We were told, and here I am to introduce you to my next quote, "Money don't grow on trees!" So we learned to be content with what we had because your mom or dad said so.

Today, it is so different. Today is designed for both parents to work to run a household smoothly. The baby boomers introduced the latchkey children/babies. Parents now trust their children to let themselves into the homes after school because mom and dad are working. So the TV, computers, cell phones, and video games have become babysitters.

JULIA BUCHANAN

Remembering the Days when TV Turned Off at Midnight

You might remember the national anthem being played before the TV went to static. During this time, it cost too much for TV stations to run for small audiences. Generally, the TV came back on around 6:00 a.m. the next day.

Chapter 17

ASSASSINATIONS, WHAT?

And yes, there were sad days too. The assassination of John F. Kennedy, his brother, Robert, and Martin Luther King Jr. just to name a few. The Vietnam War stole a lot of our young men. Women were not allowed to go to battle until 1979.

Yet those were some amazing days growing up in the '50s, '60s, and '70s.

Chapter 18

FAMOUS PEOPLE BORN DURING THOSE YEARS, WHAT?

We had some famous people who were born in the '50s and '60s: Oprah Winfrey, Stevie Wonder, Tom Hanks, Bill Murray, Dr. Phil, Denzel Washington, John Travolta, and so many more.

Chapter 19

FAMOUS ATHLETES BORN DURING THOSE YEARS, WHAT?

And sports, man, we had Walter Payton; Magic Johnson; Larry Bird; Michael Jordan; Gale Sayers; Jim Brown; and Reggie Jackson, aka Mr. October. There were more, but we'll keep that list short. These are the amazing talents born during our era. And yes, Michael Jordan was the best player ever, hands down!

Chapter 20

PICTURES, WORKBOOK, WHAT?

Everyone born during this era, I admit, didn't live their lives like ours. Some were born better off or even worse off. We didn't know that we were poor because everyone around us looked like us, lived like us. So what I have tried hard to do is capture the essence of the most. This was us! No sugarcoating our world.

Come, take a stroll down memory lane; and remember, it's okay to laugh at the way things were, but just remember after you become our age, your children will be laughing at the way things were with you too.

Then lastly, I've added a fill-in-the-blank workbook. The workbook is designed for you to participate in the fun times of yesteryear. Reminiscing and guessing what the missing word or words will be in the quote. This could be a great tool for you puzzle buffs. By writing in or guessing your response/answer, you will glean so much more into what the quote said. The jargon may stump most. But not to worry, the actually completed quotes are found in the book starting at page 59. So come along and get ready to ride the times of your life. This brings me to another quote: "Laughter…good for the soul."

MAMA SAID, WHAT?

My Mom! Nannie Beatrice Foster Porter 1911–1994. I love and miss you so much. You will live in our hearts now and forevermore.

JULIA BUCHANAN

My beautiful ninety-six-year-old mother-in-law, Teresa Traylor, 1924–2019. I love and miss you so much. You will live in our hearts now and forevermore.

MAMA SAID, WHAT?

Here's Mama Nan and six of us in 1955. *Left to right* is Hope, me, Mama holding Nellie, Faith, Lola, and you can barely see the arm of Lois.

JULIA BUCHANAN

And here all nine of us are together with Mama Nan in 1970. *Left to right, back row,* are my oldest sister Clara (9/28/55–5/7/2002), Patricia (11/5/37–11/11/2010), Lola, McDowell Jr., and me. *Front row, left to right,* Hope, Faith (11/6/47–10/7/2002), Lois, and Nellie (3/4/54–4/20/20). *Seated* is the matron herself, Nannie B., aka Mama Nan (5/30/11–1/20/1994).

Mama Said, What?

1. Mama said, "There's no such thing as bastard _____ but there are bastard parents."
2. Mama said, "They'll be _____ like this."
3. Practice what you _____.
4. You don't always get a chance to take the _____ road.
5. In time, time will _____ all. (Some say, "Heal all.")
6. I'll eat that every day of the week and twice on _____.
7. Boy, I'm _____ as a heart attack.
8. Don't just _____ about it! Be about it!
9. No telling what one will do if your _____ are against the wall.
10. Balls in your _____…now what?
11. Let he who is without _____ cast the first stone.
12. You better check yourself before you _____ yourself.
13. The apple don't _____ far from the tree.
14. The _____ you treat 'em the more they come back.
15. Don't be putting me on "_____ street."
16. We are put on this _____ not to see through one another but to see another through
17. Everybody has an _____ heel.
18. No good _____ goes unpunished.
19. _____ done right can change the world.

20. Stop learning, and you'll stop _____.
21. You scratch my _____, and I'll scratch yours.
22. The early _____ catches the worm.
23. No _____, no gain.
24. Only thing about _____ luck is it can change.
25. Better _____ than never.
26. Let _____ take its course.
27. Too afraid to _____ too scared to die.
28. I won't take you to a _____ fight.
29. Don't go after the _____ when you got the steak at home.
30. Why buy the _____ when you can get the milk for free.
31. If you don't know who your _____ are, you might end up marrying them.
32. Fool me once _____ on you, fool me twice, shame on me.
33. All _____ things must come to an end.
34. To know him was to love him, and to _____ him was to know him.
35. You're only as _____ as you feel.
36. Gee whiz boy, "what's _____ with you!"
37. _____ don't grow on trees.
38. That's just the nature of the _____.
39. Don't _____—don't tell.
40. Open a can of _____ ass.
41. It's on like _____ Kong.
42. On a wing and a _____.
43. A prayerless Christian is a _____ Christian.
44. Much prayer, much _____, little prayer, little _____, no prayer, no _____.
45. Don't _____ if you don't want the answer.
46. _____ lips sink ships.
47. It's a _____ line between love and hate.
48. You can _____ but you can't hide.
49. If these _____ could talk.

MAMA SAID, WHAT?

50. You gotta be _____ to get noticed.
51. There's a _____ to the madness.
52. Be careful what you _____ wish for, you may just get it.
53. Every _____ has a silver lining.
54. It's better to _____ than to receive.
55. They gave him the _____ degree.
56. Sometimes when you can't say something, you just _____ your hands.
57. Hey, let's go. Chop, chop_____!
58. Ain't nobody good but _____.
59. Talking _____ and saying, nothing.
60. Ain't no _____ in your game.
61. Sometimes you have to just _____ them from a distance.
62. A _____ never kiss and tell.
63. You have a memory like an _____.
64. Let's stop and address the _____ in the room.
65. _____ a bit—
66. A friend in need is a friend _____.
67. Hope springs _____.
68. Poop or get off the _____.
69. Everyone wasn't born with a _____ spoon in their mouth.
70. Are we _____? Crystal!
71. Don't put off _____ what you can do today.
72. Anything is _____ even the impossible.
73. Boy! Don't make me _____ up from here.
74. In trying _____ don't quit trying.
75. I'll knock the _____ off you.
76. Sometimes it's not the _____, sometimes its gonna rain.
77. There's a _____ sheep in every family.
78. _____ get stiches.
79. Yo _____ is mine when I get home.

80. You should _____ better…nothing else needed to be said to me.
81. You don't believe _____ meat's greasy.
82. What? You think you're _____?
83. Fool, I'll _____ you into next week.
84. I brought you in to this _____ and I'll take you out, try me.
85. Mom had me by the arm I was running/skipping in circles while she was spanking me. I said, "I won't do it again." Mom said, "Stop that crying!" I said, "How can I when you're _____ me!"
86. You can't get chicken _____ from chicken poop.
87. If you ever call the police on me, you'd better find another _____ to live on.
88. It is _____ it is.
89. I would ask my dad what was for dinner, and he would tell me, "Catch medicine." I asked him, "What is that?" His response, "None of your damn _____!"
90. Don't count your _____ before they hatch.
91. Don't put all your _____ in one basket.
92. One bad _____ can spoil the whole bushel.
93. One man's food is another man's _____.
94. "Hold your _____ out!"
95. Don't let the _____ catch your ass not at home.
96. Don't let your mouth write a check that your _____ can't cash.
97. You hard of hearing? Get that damn _____ roll out of your ears fool!
98. Your _____ sense wouldn't even fill a thimble.
99. Go find me something to _____ your ass with (that was a long walk).
100. My hearing is so good that I could hear a cat _____ on cotton.
101. Sunshine is the _____ disinfectant.

102. Everyone you meet is _____ a personal battle you know nothing about.
103. The family that _____ together stays together.
104. Big _____ watching
105. _____ on the things you can control makes the things you can't less scary.
106. _____ tomorrow's regret.
107. A man's _____ flows from the same well as his weakness.
108. _____ doesn't strike in the same place twice.
109. A _____ in time saves nine.
110. _____ good for the soul.
111. You're just too good for your _____ good.
112. The _____ is on the wall.
113. You want to know me? Come walk in my _____ for a mile.
114. Fear doesn't solve _____. Hope does.
115. A _____ is only as strong as its weakest link.
116. A _____ can't change its spots.
117. A watched _____ or pot never boils.
118. _____ speak louder than words.
119. An _____ a day keeps the doctor away.
120. An ounce of prevention is better that a _____ of cure.
121. You make your _____ you got to sleep in it.
122. Birds of a _____ flock together.
123. _____ thicker than water.
124. _____ begins at home.
125. _____ killed the cat.
126. Cold hands, warm _____.
127. Cleanliness is next to _____.
128. _____ doesn't pay.
129. Do as I _____ and not as I do.
130. Say what you _____ and _____ what you say.

131. If you can't say something _____ then don't say nothing.
132. Do not cut off your _____ to spite your face.
133. Don't judge a _____ by its cover.
134. Stop making a _____ out of a mole hill.
135. Don't throw your _____ to swine.
136. Do unto _____ as you would have them do unto you.
137. It's easier _____ than done.
138. Every _____ has its day.
139. Girl, gimme the _____.
140. Everybody wants to go to _____, but nobody wants to die.
141. Good things _____ to those who wait.
142. Finder's keepers _____ weepers.
143. First impressions are the most lasting.
144. _____ will get you nowhere.
145. Give a man enough _____, he'll hang himself.
146. _____ helps those who helps themselves.
147. Haste makes _____.
148. He who hesitates is _____.
149. Hell has no _____ like a woman's scorn.
150. _____ is always twenty-twenty.
151. _____ is where the heart is.
152. Honesty is the _____ policy.
153. Hope for the _____ but prepare for the worst.
154. If anything can go _____, it will.
155. If at _____ you don't succeed, try and try again.
156. If it ain't _____ don't fix it.
157. If you can't _____ 'em join 'em.
158. _____ are like butt holes, everyone has one.
159. As long as I owe you, you'll never be _____.
160. If you lie down with _____, you will get up with fleas.
161. You play with _____ you will get burned.

162. If you can't stand the _____, get out of the kitchen.
163. If you got it, _____ it.
164. _____ is bliss.
165. _____: "Tools of incompetence, used to build monuments of nothingness. And those who specializes in them are seldom good at anything else."
166. It ain't over 'til the fat _____ sings.
167. In every _____ a little rain must fall.
168. It's no use _____ over spilled milk.
169. It takes a whole _____ to raise a child.
170. It takes one to _____ one.
171. It takes two to _____.
172. Keep your friends close and your _____ closer.
173. Laugh and the _____ laughs with you. Cry and you cry alone.
174. Sweetheart, find your joy in your _____ in Jesus Christ.
175. Let _____ be bygones.
176. Its best if you just _____ well enough alone.
177. Like _____, like son.
178. Live and _____ live.
179. _____ before you leap.
180. The love of _____ is the root of all evil.
181. Don't look a gift _____ in his mouth.
182. Never _____ never.
183. There's no _____ for the wicked.
184. No news is _____ news.
185. Nothing is certain but death and _____.
186. Oil and water do not _____
187. One man's _____ is another man's treasure
188. Opportunity only _____ once.
189. Out of _____, out of mind.
190. The _____ isn't always greener on the other side.
191. Practice makes _____.

192. Boy, you're preaching to the _____.
193. Put your _____ where your mouth is.
194. Respect is not _____ its earned.
195. Sticks and stones may break my _____, but words will never hurt me.
196. _____ is cheap.
197. Tell the truth _____ the devil.
198. The light is on, but nobody is _____
199. It's the last _____ that broke the camel's back.
200. The way to a man's _____ is through his stomach.
201. There is always an _____ to the rule.
202. There's more _____ in the sea.
203. There's more than one way to _____ a cat.
204. There's no place like _____.
205. Where there is smoke, there's _____.
206. There is _____ in numbers.
207. Only _____ will tell.
208. Heavy lies the _____ that wears the crown.
209. The _____ sometimes hurt.
210. To err is human, to forgive is _____.
211. Too many _____ spoil the broth.
212. Two _____ are better than one.
213. You can kill two _____ with one stone.
214. Two is company, three is a _____.
215. Two _____ don't make it right.
216. Use it or _____ it.
217. Variety is the spice of _____.
218. Up a _____ without a paddle.
219. _____ softly but carry a big stick.
220. Walls have _____.
221. What does not _____ you make you strong.
222. What comes around _____ around.
223. Whatever floats your _____.
224. When it rains, it _____.
225. Where there's a _____, there's a way.

MAMA SAID, WHAT?

226. You are never too old to _____.
227. You can bring the _____ to water, but you can't make him drink.
228. You cannot get _____ from a turnip.
229. You can't _____ them all.
230. _____ up or shut up.
231. It's a poor _____ that won't wag his own tail.
232. Sometimes you have to _____ up something in order to get something.
233. Those that can't do, _____.
234. Mama said, "Don't _____ with someone when you know you're right!"
235. It's _____ way of the highway.
236. Friends with _____ don't make no damn sense.
237. Come on and _____ like you got some "ACT LIKE" in you!
238. Everything that _____ ain't gold.
239. _____, busted and disgusted.
240. What you don't know won't _____ you.
241. When you point a _____, just remember three are pointing right back at you.
242. When you fight fire with fire sometimes you get _____.
243. _____ before you speak.
244. Open _____ insert foot.
245. "Anyone can love when it's easy but if we love when its _____, then we are all the better."
246. _____ is good for the soul.
247. Sometimes we only _____ what we want to _____.
248. If you want to hear God _____ just tell Him what you have planned.
249. Wow, you put your _____ in it this time.
250. He who laughs first laughs _____.
251. Eye for an _____ and a tooth for a _____.

47

252. Don't _____ nothing won't be nothing.
253. For every _____ there's a reaction.
254. Prayer is the key to heaven. Faith _____ the door.
255. Beauty is in the _____ of the beholder.
256. _____ is only skin deep.
257. I'm not _____, I'm just saying.
258. A hard _____ makes a soft behind.
259. Go with the _____.
260. Misery _____ company.
261. Necessity is the mother of _____.
262. It's not the circumstances that create the _____, it's you.
263. The chickens have come home to _____.
264. Step out on _____.
265. Tough times don't last long, but tough _____ do.
266. Some grow old but not _____.
267. _____ don't make friends.
268. The _____ is in the pudding.
269. The needs of the many _____ the needs of the few.
270. No man is an _____.
271. Jack of all trades, _____ of none.
272. _____ it will be, it will be.
273. You can't _____ a stick if it's in a bundle.
274. Once you take your feet off the gas, you get left in the _____.
275. Somebody ought to do something about this. That _____ is you.
276. When you _____ better you do better.
277. Never ever _____ four things in your life: trust, promise, relation, and heart
278. You don't always take a seat and eat at other people's _____.
279. Don't always _____ what you see.

280. Don't always take the _____ less traveled.
281. Take the high _____.
282. When life hands you _____, make lemonade.
283. A lazy _____ is a dead weight.
284. Individuals play the game but _____ beat the odds.
285. You don't go as far as you _____. You go as far as your team.
286. _____ is of the essence.
287. "It's an old family secret!" If I tell you I'll have to _____ you.
288. _____ of a different color.
289. When God closes a door, He opens a _____.
290. Anything that doesn't _____ breaks.
291. An _____ mind is a devil's workshop.
292. People who live in _____ houses shouldn't throw stones.
293. Only the _____ survive.
294. You can cover up ugly with lipstick, but you can't cover up _____ because it always speaks through.
295. Many _____ make light work.
296. Perfection is the _____ lie.
297. Flight, _____ or freeze
298. Even when you tickle a _____ the right way even he has to laugh
299. Always try to bring _____ to the chaos.
300. "The English language is like a tall cold _____. It's always better with a little twang in it."
301. Grease the hand but don't _____ the hand that feeds you.
302. We're all born into a role but the person you _____ is up to you.
303. When you _____ say something, you're saying something.
304. Man is key. Woman is door to let new _____ in.

305. Courtesy given is courtesy _____.
306. Good _____ over evil.
307. _____: Protects fools, little children, and drunkards.
308. Iron _____ iron.
309. Be nice to those you meet on the way _____. They're the same folks you'll meet on the way _____.
310. Sometimes we are not the masters over our circumstances, but we can always master our response that _____ is ours.
311. A wise man said, "Never move anything into an _____ you can't carry out in one box."
312. Own your own _____, don't let it own you.
313. "Unpleasant things don't go away just because you close your eyes or choose to remain ignorant of them. It doesn't alter their reality but awareness of them can help us to be _____ and more prudent in our behavior" (Kay Arthur).
314. Don't be too _____ for our own good.
315. Mama said, "Always make sure to wear clean underwear just in case you have to go to the _____."
316. Don't _____ the small stuff.
317. You don't miss the water until the wells run dry.
318. It's water under the _____.
319. Let sleeping _____ lie.
320. It's nothing to write _____ about.
321. Shut the _____ door.
322. _____ yet so far away.
323. _____ there, done that.
324. What goes _____ must come down.
325. What's for _____, ma? "Sawdust and rats."
326. What's for _____, ma? "Frog eyes and jello."
327. You're just a _____ for punishment.
328. Fall on your _____.
329. Get down with the _____ nitty gritty.

330. Lights on but nobody _____.
331. With _____ comes wisdom.
332. With great _____ comes great responsibility.
333. For a while they were _____ like flies.
334. Float to the top or sink to the bottom, everything in the _____ is the churn.
335. Why do bad things happen to _____ people?
336. Nothing ventured, nothing _____.
337. If you fight with _____ too long you could become one.
338. Tears don't move God, _____ does.
339. _____ is not an option.
340. It ain't _____ until it's ova!
341. You're just too _____ for your own britches.
342. There's _____ at the end of the tunnel.
343. Not all _____ is good money.
344. You don't bring a _____ to a gun fight.
345. Ain't that the pot calling the _____ black.
346. The best things in life are worth _____ for.
347. The best things in _____ aren't free.
348. Poor is a state of _____.
349. If you feel like you're _____ you are.
350. If you _____ it you can believe it.
351. _____ heals all wounds.
352. One _____ don't stop no show.
353. Grass don't get a chance to grow under your _____.
354. Winners anticipate, losers _____.
355. Disappoint your _____.
356. Be the _____ of your life not the reactor.
357. We can all be _____.
358. _____ knows my heart
359. "God promises peace not the absence of _____" (Pastor Mike Todd TC Church).
360. "_____" where every day is howdy, howdy and there will never be a goodbye.

361. _____ is the thief of time.
362. What's good for the goose is good for the _____.
363. See? This is one _____ here that we ain't fitna do.
364. Everyone has a _____, but not everyone will see one.
365. Boy! You ain't worth a _____ nickel.
366. When the going gets _____ the _____ gets going.
367. A _____ ride beats a dressed up walk any day.
368. Sometimes it ain't worth _____ about…just keep on moving.
369. Do I look like, Booboo the _____ to you?
370. Boy! My _____!
371. A _____ of three strands ain't easily broken.
372. If you want something done _____ sometimes you have to do it yourself.
373. Check the _____ not the seed.
374. _____ can't be choosy.
375. Jumped from the frying pan into the _____.
376. No amount of money bought a _____ of time.
377. There are always two sides to every _____.
378. Waste not, _____ not.
379. That came _____ from the horse's mouth.
380. Never stop _____ what seems unattainable.
381. He who has nothing has nothing to _____.
382. You're gonna _____ me when I'm gone.
383. How many times have you caught yourself saying, "To make a _____ story, short."
384. "It's not the load that _____ you. It's the way you carry it" (Lena Horne).
385. Throwing _____ to the wind.
386. "People forget what you say, but they _____ how you made them feel" (Warren Beatty).
387. It's what you do after you lose everything that _____ who you really are.

MAMA SAID, WHAT?

388. What you _____ you perfect.
389. Can't make the _____ if you don't take the shot.
390. Life's only certainties are death and _____.
391. Sometimes I feel like I'm just talking to the _____.
392. See you later alligator, afterwhile _____.
393. I was old when I was _____.
394. It's been a plum, pleasing, pleasure to _____ you.
395. I'm having a _____ moment.
396. Pick it up and keep it _____.
397. _____ makes the heart grow fonder.
398. Association brings about _____.
399. _____ people, hurt people.
400. _____ is just a number.
401. Let's just _____ to disagree.
402. It's a tough _____ but somebody's got to do it.
403. "You can't get away from _____ by moving from one place to another" (Ernest Hemingway).
404. He's calling _____ (hanging over toilet vomiting).
405. Grow some thick _____ skin.
406. Rest your _____ child, rest your heart.
407. There are starving children in _____, you better eat your food.
408. Head 'em up, move 'em out _____!
409. Give a man a fish and he'll eat for a day. But _____ a man to fish and he'll eat for a lifetime.
410. Give you an _____ and you'll take a mile.
411. How do you see that _____? Half empty or half full?
412. Remember, you're no spring _____ anymore.
413. _____ your food/candy? Three-second rule. Kiss it up to God and eat it.

53

JULIA BUCHANAN

414. You'd forget your head if it wasn't connected to your _____.
415. That's my _____, and I'm sticking to it.
416. If I've told you once I've told you a _____ times.
417. Remember when you're pointing your _____, three are pointing right back at you.
418. Children are like _____, soaking up whatever they hear or see.
419. Don't let the _____ hit you where the dog should've bit you.
420. You know if you keep _____ the same dumb stuff, you'll keep getting the same dumb results.
421. Say that again, and I'll have to wash your mouth out with _____.
422. Don't let the kids _____ your love affairs.
423. It's raining, and you're not made of sugar so you won't _____.
424. God answers _____ three ways: yes, no, and wait.
425. This hurts me _____ than it will hurt you.
426. _____! Look! And listen!
427. Well, you can't have your _____ and eat it too.
428. One _____ don't stop no show.
429. Over my _____ body!
430. You're getting on my _____ nerve.
431. Like _____ like daughter.
432. I'm doing this for your own _____.
433. I'm doing this for your own _____.
434. You're gonna get ten lashes with a _____ noodle.
435. Girl you're just _____ the fat.
436. If your friends jump off a _____ are you going to follow them.
437. Dare to be _____.

54

438. Red, yellow, black, or white we are all _____ in God's sight.
439. An honest day's _____ for an honest day's pay.
440. Life's _____ pleasure…chocolate.
441. Living the life of _____.
442. When your knees start rocking, _____ on them.
443. Going for _____.
444. _____ makes the dream work.
445. A dream without _____ is just a hallucination.
446. The world is paved with good _____.
447. Friends…they come a _____ a dozen.
448. Never let your schooling get in the way of your _____.
449. I won't be _____ when you aim high and miss but I will be when you aim low and hit (Michael Angelo).
450. Showing your _____ colors.
451. If you think you can or you think you can't, you're _____ (Henry Ford).
452. Be an hour early than a _____ late.
453. Aristotle said you are what you repeatedly _____.
454. Never embarrass your _____.
455. Happy _____ happy life.
456. It's on a need-to-know _____ and you don't need to know.
457. Good things come in _____ packages.
458. You want to make an _____ find your broom.
459. Always _____ for the stars.
460. If it walks like a duck and _____ like a duck, it's a duck.
461. Move from in front of the television, your daddy wasn't no _____ maker.

462. Stop running in and out of this house letting all of my _____ out.
463. Try putting the _____ on the other feet.
464. You better _____ while you're ahead.
465. Passing the _____.
466. Be careful how you treat _____ going up because they're the same ones you meet coming down.
467. Don't put your _____ ahead of the greater good.
468. Those are just the _____ of the trade.
469. Leave your _____ in God's hands.
470. Sometimes it's just a _____ to an end.
471. If the _____ fits wear it.
472. It's your animal magnetism, you attract _____.
473. Don't play me _____.
474. _____ is caring.
475. Let the _____ fall where they may.
476. We don't _____ a man when he's down.
477. All _____ things come to an end.
478. Experience is the best _____.
479. Man, it was right on the _____ of my tongue.
480. Success: Those who say it can't be done are being _____ by those doing it!
481. _____ to pray is what gives you the strength to stand.
482. Feed your fears and your _____ will starve.
483. Feed you _____ and your fears will starve.
484. Don't _____ the fence, all in or all out.
485. It's not the size of the man in the _____; it's the size of the _____ in the man.
486. Just a _____ off the old block.
487. Even a blind _____ finds a nut sometimes.
488. Go where you're _____ not tolerated.
489. _____ makes you the most beautiful person in the world no matter what you look like.

490. God wants you to walk then the devil sends a _____.
491. _____: Christ Offers forgiveness for everyone, everywhere.
492. _____ company ruins good morals.
493. Nothing from nothing _____ nothing.
494. _____ should be like books, few but hand selected.
495. Life is a party so _____ it.
496. Don't ever let another mother's child cost you your _____.
497. Information just seems to go in one _____ and out the other.
498. _____ can't hide his stripes for too long.
499. It's not how you start it's how you _____.
500. Don't wake up a _____ giant.

Mama Said, What?

1. Mama said, "There's no such thing as bastard children but there are bastard parents."
2. Mama said, "They'll be days like this."
3. Practice what you preach.
4. You don't always get a chance to take the high road.
5. In time, time will tell all. (Some say, "Heal all.")
6. I'll eat that every day of the week and twice on Sunday.
7. Boy, I'm serious as a heart attack.
8. Don't just talk about it! Be about it!
9. No telling what one will do if your backs are against the wall
10. Balls in your court…now what?
11. Let he who is without sin cast the first stone.
12. You better check yourself before you wreck yourself.
13. The apple don't fall far from the tree.
14. The worse you treat 'em the more they come back.
15. Don't be putting me on "front street."
16. We are put on this earth not to see through one another but to see another through.
17. Everybody has an Achilles' heel.
18. No good deed goes unpunished.
19. Love done right can change the world.
20. Stop learning, and you'll stop growing.
21. You scratch my back, and I'll scratch yours.
22. The early bird catches the worm.
23. No pain, no gain.
24. Only thing about luck is it can change.
25. Better late than never.

26. Let nature take its course.
27. Too afraid to live too scared to die.
28. I won't take you to a dog fight.
29. Don't go after the hamburger when you got the steak at home.
30. Why buy the cow when you can get the milk for free.
31. If you don't know who your relatives are, you might end up marrying them.
32. Fool me once shame on you, fool me twice, shame on me.
33. All good things must come to an end.
34. To know him was to love him and to love him was to know him.
35. You're only as old as you feel.
36. Gee whiz boy, "What's wrong with you!"
37. Money don't grow on trees.
38. That's just the nature of the beast.
39. Don't ask—don't tell
40. Open a can of whoop ass.
41. It's on like Donkey Kong.
42. On a wing and a prayer.
43. A prayerless Christian is a powerless Christian.
44. Much prayer, much power, little prayer, little power, no prayer, no power.
45. Don't ask if you don't want the answer.
46. Loose lips sink ships.
47. It's a thin line between love and hate.
48. You can run but you can't hide.
49. If these walls could talk.
50. You gotta be seen to get noticed.
51. There's a method to the madness.
52. Be careful what you wish for, you may just get it.
53. Every cloud has a silver lining.
54. It's better to give than to receive.
55. They gave him the third degree.

56. Sometimes when you can't say something you just wave your hands.
57. Hey, let's go. Chop, chop hurry!
58. Ain't nobody good but God.
59. Talking loud and saying, nothing.
60. Ain't no shame in your game.
61. Sometimes you have to just love them from a distance.
62. A gentleman never kiss and tell.
63. You have a memory like an elephant.
64. Let's stop and address the elephant in the room.
65. Karma's a bit—
66. A friend in need is a friend indeed.
67. Hope springs eternal.
68. Poop or get off the pot.
69. Everyone wasn't born with a silver spoon in their mouth.
70. Are we clear? Crystal!
71. Don't put off tomorrow what you can do today.
72. Anything is possible even the impossible.
73. Boy! Don't make me get up from here.
74. In trying times don't quit trying.
75. I'll knock the black off you.
76. Sometimes it's not the sunshine, sometimes it's gonna rain.
77. There's a black sheep in every family.
78. Snitches get stitches.
79. Yo ass is mine when I get home.
80. You should know better…nothing else needed to be said to me
81. You don't believe fat meat's greasy.
82. What? You think you're grown?
83. Fool, I'll knock you into next week.
84. I brought you into this world and I'll take you out, try me.
85. Mom had me by the arm. I was running/skipping in circles while she was spanking me. I said, "I won't do it

again." Mom said, "Stop that crying!" I said, "How can I when you're beating me!"
86. You can't get chicken stew from chicken poop.
87. If you ever call the police on me, you'd better find another planet to live on.
88. It is what it is.
89. I would ask my dad what was for dinner and he would tell me, "Catch medicine." I asked him, "What is that?" His response, "None of your damn business!"
90. Don't count your chickens before they hatch.
91. Don't put all your eggs in one basket.
92. One bad apple can spoil the whole bushel.
93. One man's food is another man's poison.
94. "Hold your brains out!"
95. Don't let the streetlights catch your ass, not at home.
96. Don't let your mouth write a check that your ass can't cash.
97. You hard of hearing? #! Get that damn tootsie roll out of your ears fool!
98. Your common sense wouldn't even fill a thimble.
99. Go find me something to beat your ass with (that was a long walk.)
100. My hearing is so good that I could hear a cat piss on cotton.
101. Sunshine is the best disinfectant.
102. Everyone you meet is fighting a personal battle you know nothing about.
103. The family that prays together stays together.
104. Big brother's watching.
105. Focus on the things you can control makes the things you can't less scary.
106. Sin—tomorrow's regret.
107. A man's strength flows from the same well as his weakness.
108. Lightning doesn't strike in the same place twice.
109. A stitch in time saves nine.
110. Laughter is good for the soul.

111. You're just too good for your own good.
112. The handwriting is on the wall.
113. You want to know me? Come walk in my shoes for a mile.
114. Fear doesn't solve problems. Hope does
115. A chain is only as strong as its weakest link.
116. A leopard can't change its spots.
117. A watched kettle or pot never boils.
118. Actions speak louder than words.
119. An apple a day keeps the doctor away.
120. An ounce of prevention is better than a pound of cure.
121. You make your bed you got to sleep in it.
122. Birds of a feather flock together.
123. Blood's thicker than water.
124. Charity begins at home.
125. Curiosity killed the cat.
126. Cold hands, warm heart.
127. Cleanliness is next to godliness.
128. Crime doesn't pay.
129. Do as I say and not as I do.
130. Say what you mean and mean what you say.
131. If you can't say something nice, then don't say nothing.
132. Do not cut off your nose to spite your face.
133. Don't judge a book by its cover.
134. Stop making a mountain out of a molehill.
135. Don't throw your pearls to swine.
136. Do unto others as you would have them do unto you.
137. It's easier said than done.
138. Every dog has its day.
139. Girl, gimme the 4-1-1.
140. Everybody wants to go to heaven but nobody wants to die.
141. Good things come to those who wait.
142. Finders keepers losers weepers.
143. First impressions are the most lasting.
144. Flattery will get you nowhere.

145. Give a man enough rope, he'll hang himself.
146. God helps those who help themselves.
147. Haste makes waste.
148. He who hesitates is lost.
149. Hell has no fury like a woman's scorn.
150. Hindsight is always twenty-twenty.
151. Home is where the heart is.
152. Honesty is the best policy.
153. Hope for the best but prepare for the worst.
154. If anything can go wrong, it will.
155. If at first you don't succeed, try, try again.
156. If it ain't broke don't fix it.
157. If you can't beat 'em join 'em.
158. Opinions are like butt holes, everyone has one.
159. As long as I owe you, you'll never be broke.
160. If you lie down with dogs, you will get up with fleas.
161. You play with fire you will get burned.
162. If you can't stand the heat get out of the kitchen.
163. If you got it, flaunt it.
164. Ignorance is bliss.
165. Excuses: "Tools of incompetence, used to build monuments of nothingness. And those who specialize in them are seldom good at anything else."
166. It ain't over 'til the fat lady sings.
167. In every life, a little rain must fall.
168. It's no use crying over spilled milk.
169. It takes a whole village to raise a child.
170. It takes one to know one.
171. It takes two to tangle.
172. Keep your friends close and your enemies closer.
173. Laugh and the world laughs with you. Cry and you cry alone.
174. Sweetheart, find your joy in your faith in Jesus Christ.
175. Let bygones be bygones.
176. It's best if you just leave well enough alone.
177. Like father, like son.

178. Live and let live.
179. Look before you leap.
180. The love of money is the root of all evil.
181. Don't look a gift horse in his mouth.
182. Never say never.
183. There's no rest for the wicked.
184. No news is good news.
185. Nothing is certain but death and taxes.
186. Oil and water do not mix.
187. One man's trash is another man's treasure.
188. Opportunity only knocks once.
189. Out of sight, out of mind.
190. The grass isn't always greener on the other side.
191. Practice makes perfect.
192. Boy, you're preaching to the choir.
193. Put your money where your mouth is.
194. Respect is not given it's earned.
195. Sticks and stones may break my bones, but words will never hurt me.
196. Talk is cheap.
197. Tell the truth shame the devil.
198. The light is on but nobody is home.
199. It's the last straw that broke the camel's back.
200. The way to a man's heart is through his stomach.
201. There is always an exception to the rule.
202. There's more fish in the sea.
203. There's more than one way to skin a cat.
204. There's no place like home.
205. Where there is smoke, there's fire.
206. There is safety in numbers.
207. Only time will tell.
208. Heavy lies the head that wears the crown.
209. The truth sometimes hurts.
210. To err is human, to forgive is divine.
211. Too many cooks spoil the broth.
212. Two heads are better than one.

213. You can kill two birds with one stone.
214. Two is a company, three is a crowd.
215. Two wrongs don't make it right.
216. Use it or lose it.
217. Variety is the spice of life.
218. Up a creek without a paddle.
219. Walk softly but carry a big stick.
220. Walls have ears.
221. What does not kill you makes you strong.
222. What comes around goes around.
223. Whatever floats your boat.
224. When it rains it pours.
225. Where there's a will, there's a way.
226. You are never too old to learn.
227. You can bring the horse to water but you can't make him drink.
228. You cannot get blood from a turnip.
229. You can't win them all.
230. Put up or shut up.
231. It's a poor dog that won't wag his own tail.
232. Sometimes you have to give up something in order to get something.
233. Those that can't do, teach.
234. Mama said, "Don't argue with someone when you know you're right!"
235. It's my way or the highway.
236. Friends with benefits don't make no damn sense.
237. Come on and move like you got some "ACT LIKE" in you!
238. Everything that glitters ain't gold.
239. Broke, busted, and disgusted.
240. What you don't know won't hurt you.
241. When you point a finger, just remember three are pointing right back at you.
242. When you fight fire with fire sometimes you get burned.
243. Think before you speak.
244. Open mouth insert foot.

245. "Anyone can love when it's easy, but if we love when it's hard, then we are all the better."
246. Confession is good for the soul.
247. Sometimes we only hear what we want to hear.
248. If you want to hear God laugh just tell Him what you have planned.
249. Wow, you put your foot in it this time.
250. He who laughs first laughs best.
251. Eye for an eye and a tooth for a tooth.
252. Don't start nothing won't be nothing.
253. For every action, there's a reaction.
254. Prayer is the key to heaven. Faith unlocks the door.
255. Beauty is in the eye of the beholder.
256. Beauty is only skin deep.
257. I'm not hating, I'm just saying.
258. A hard head makes a soft behind.
259. Go with the flow.
260. Misery loves company.
261. Necessity is the mother of invention.
262. It's not the circumstances that create the joy, it's you.
263. The chickens have come home to roost.
264. Step out on faith.
265. Tough times don't last long but tough people do.
266. Some grow old but not up.
267. Secrets don't make friends.
268. The proof is in the pudding.
269. The needs of the many outweigh the needs of the few.
270. No man is an island.
271. Jack of all trades, master of none.
272. If it will be, it will be.
273. You can't break a stick if it's in a bundle.
274. Once you take your feet off the gas you get left in the dusk.
275. Somebody ought to do something about this. That somebody is you.
276. When you know better you do better.

277. Never ever break four things in your life: trust, promise, relation, and heart.
278. You don't always take a seat and eat at other people's table.
279. Don't always trust what you see.
280. Don't always take the road less traveled.
281. Take the high road.
282. When life hands you lemons make lemonade.
283. A lazy weight is a dead weight.
284. Individuals play the game, but teams beat the odds.
285. You don't go as far as you dream. You go as far as your team
286. Time is of the essence.
287. "It's an old family secret!" If I tell you I'll have to kill you.
288. Horse of a different color.
289. When God closes a door. He opens a window.
290. Anything that doesn't bend, breaks.
291. An idle mind is a devil's workshop.
292. People who live in glass houses shouldn't throw stones.
293. Only the strong survive.
294. You can cover up ugly with lipstick but you can't cover up stupid because it always speaks through.
295. Many hands make light work.
296. Perfection is the perfect lie.
297. Flight, fight, or freeze.
298. Even when you tickle a grinch the right way even he has to laugh.
299. Always try to bring calm to the chaos.
300. "The English language is like a tall cold lemonade it's always better with a little twang in it."
301. Grease the hand but don't bite the hand that feeds you.
302. We're all born into a role but the person you become is up to you.
303. When you don't say something, you're saying something.
304. Man is key. Woman is door to let new life in.
305. Courtesy given is courtesy returned.
306. Good triumphs over evil.

307. Fate: Protects fools, little children, and drunkards.
308. Iron sharpens iron.
309. Be nice to those you meet on the way up. They're the same folks you'll meet on the way down.
310. Sometimes we are not the masters over our circumstances, but we can always master our response…that choice is ours.
311. A wise man said, "never move anything into an office you can't carry out in one box."
312. Own your own destiny, don't let it own you.
313. "Unpleasant things don't go away just because you close your eyes or choose to remain ignorant of them. It doesn't alter their reality but awareness of them can help us to be wiser and more prudent in our behavior" (Kay Arthur).
314. Don't be too smart for our own good.
315. Mama said, "Always make sure to wear clean underwear just in case you have to go to the hospital."
316. Don't sweat the small stuff.
317. You don't miss the water until the wells run dry.
318. It's water under the bridge.
319. Let sleeping dogs lie.
320. It's nothing to write home about.
321. Shut the front door.
322. Close yet so far away.
323. Been there, done that.
324. What goes up must come down.
325. What's for dinner, ma? "Sawdust and rats."
326. What's for dessert, ma? "Frog eyes and jello."
327. You're just a glutton for punishment.
328. Fall on your sword.
329. Get down with the real nitty-gritty.
330. Lights on but nobody home.
331. With age comes wisdom.
332. With great power comes great responsibility.
333. For a while, they were dropping like flies.

334. Float to the top or sink to the bottom, everything in the middle is the churn.
335. Why do bad things happen to good people?
336. Nothing ventured…nothing gained.
337. If you fight with monsters too long you could become one.
338. Tears don't move God, faith does.
339. Failure is not an option.
340. It ain't over until it's ova!
341. You're just too smart for your own britches.
342. There's light at the end of the tunnel.
343. Not all money is good money.
344. You don't bring a knife to a gunfight.
345. Ain't that the pot calling the kettle black.
346. The best things in life are worth waiting for.
347. The best things in life aren't free.
348. Poor is a state of mind.
349. If you feel like you're rich you are.
350. If you see it you can believe it.
351. Time heals all wounds.
352. One monkey don't stop no show.
353. Grass don't get a chance to grow under your feet.
354. Winners anticipate, losers react.
355. Disappoint your disappointment.
356. Be the creator of your life, not the reactor.
357. We can all be heroes.
358. God knows my heart.
359. "God promises peace, not the absence of pressure" (Pastor Mike Todd TC Church).
360. "Heaven" where every day is howdy, howdy and there will never be a goodbye.
361. Procrastination is the thief of time.
362. What's good for the goose is good for the gander.
363. See? This is one thing here that we ain't fitna do.
364. Everyone has a chance but not everyone will see one.
365. Boy! You ain't worth a plug nickel.

366. When the going gets tough the tough get going.
367. A raggedy ride beats a dressed-up walk any day.
368. Sometimes it ain't worth complaining about…just keep on moving.
369. Do I look like, Booboo the fool to you?
370. Boy! My bad!
371. A cord of three strands ain't easily broken.
372. If you want something done right sometimes you have to do it yourself.
373. Check the soil not the seed.
374. Beggars can't be choosy.
375. Jumped from the frying pan into the fire.
376. No amount of money bought a second of time.
377. There are always two sides to every story.
378. Waste not, want not.
379. That came straight from the horse's mouth.
380. Never stop seeking what seems unattainable.
381. He who has nothing has nothing to lose.
382. You're gonna miss me when I'm gone.
383. How many times have you caught yourself saying, "To make a long story, short."
384. "It's not the load that breaks you it's the way you carry it" (Lena Horne).
385. Throwing caution to the wind.
386. "People forget what you say, but they remember how you made them feel" (Warren Beatty).
387. It's what you do after you lose everything that defines who you really are.
388. What you practice you perfect.
389. Can't make the goal if you don't take the shot.
390. Life's only certainties are death and taxes.
391. Sometimes I feel like I'm just talking to the wall.
392. See you later alligator, afterwhile crocodile.
393. I was old when I was young.
394. It's been a plum, pleasing, pleasure to meet you.
395. I'm having a senior moment.

396. Pick it up and keep it moving.
397. Absence makes the heart grow fonder.
398. Association brings about assimilation
399. Hurt people, hurt people.
400. Age is just a number.
401. Let's just agree to disagree.
402. It's a tough job, but somebody's got to do it.
403. "You can't get away from yourself by moving from one place to another" (Ernest Hemingway).
404. He's calling Earl (hanging over toilet vomiting).
405. Grow some thick skin.
406. Rest your heart child, rest your heart.
407. There are starving children in Africa, you better eat your food.
408. Head 'em up, move 'em out Rawhide!
409. Give a man a fish and he'll eat for a day. But teach a man to fish and he'll eat for a lifetime.
410. Give you an inch and you'll take a mile.
411. How do you see that glass? Half empty or half full?
412. Remember, you're no spring chicken anymore.
413. Dropped your food/candy? Three-second rule. Kiss it up to God and eat it.
414. You'd forget your head if it wasn't connected to your shoulders.
415. That's my story and I'm sticking to it.
416. If I've told you once I've told you a thousand times.
417. Remember when you're pointing your finger, three are pointing right back at you.
418. Children are like sponges, soaking up whatever they hear or see.
419. Don't let the doorknob hit you where the dog should've bit you.
420. You know if you keep doing the same dumb stuff, you'll keep getting the same dumb results.
421. Say that again, and I'll have to wash your mouth out with soap.

422. Don't let the kids dictate your love affairs.
423. It's raining and you're not made of sugar so you won't melt.
424. God answers prayers three ways: yes, no, and wait.
425. This hurts me more than it will hurt you.
426. Stop! Look! And listen!
427. Well, you can't have your cake and eat it too.
428. Don't let one bad apple spoil the whole bunch.
429. One monkey don't stop no show.
430. Over my dead body!
431. You're getting on my last nerve.
432. Like mother like daughter.
433. I'm doing this for your own good.
434. You're gonna get ten lashes with a wet noodle.
435. Girl, you're just chewing the fat.
436. If your friends jump off a cliff are you going to follow them.
437. Dare to be different.
438. Red, yellow, black, or white we are all precious in God's sight.
439. An honest day's work for an honest day's pay
440. Life's guilty pleasure…chocolate.
441. Living the life of Riley.
442. When your knees start rocking, kneel on them.
443. Going for broke.
444. Teamwork makes the dream work.
445. A dream without action is just a hallucination.
446. The world is paved with good intentions.
447. Friends…they come a dime a dozen.
448. Never let your schooling get in the way of your education.
449. I won't be disappointed when you aim high and miss but I will be when you aim low and hit (Michael Angelo).
450. Showing your true colors.
451. If you think you can or you think you can't, you're right (Henry Ford).
452. Be an hour early than a minute late.

453. Aristotle said you are what you repeatedly do.
454. Never embarrass your mama.
455. Happy wife, happy life.
456. It's on a need-to-know basis and you don't need to know.
457. Good things come in small packages.
458. You want to make an impact, find your broom.
459. Always shoot for the stars.
460. If it walks like a duck and quack like a duck, it's a duck.
461. Move from in front of the TV, your daddy wasn't no glassmaker.
462. Stop running in and out of this house, letting all of my heat out.
463. Try putting the shoe on the other feet.
464. You better quit while you're ahead.
465. Passing the buck.
466. Be careful how you treat people going up because they're the same ones you meet coming down.
467. Don't put your needs ahead of the greater good.
468. Those are just the tricks of the trade.
469. Leave your enemies in God's hands.
470. Sometimes it's just a means to an end.
471. If the shoe fits, wear it.
472. It's your animal magnetism, you attract animals.
473. Don't play me cheap.
474. Sharing is caring.
475. Let the chips fall where they may.
476. We don't kick a man when he's down.
477. All good things come to an end.
478. Experience is the best teacher.
479. Man, it was right on the tip of my tongue.
480. Success: Those who say it can't be done are being passed by those doing it!
481. Kneeling to pray is what gives you the strength to stand.
482. Feed your fears and your faith will starve.
483. Feed you faith and your fears will starve.
484. Don't straddle the fence, all in or all out.

485. It's not the size of the man in the fight; it's the size of the fight in the man.
486. Just a chip off the old block.
487. Even a blind squirrel finds a nut sometimes.
488. Go where you're celebrated, not tolerated.
489. Kindness makes you the most beautiful person in the world, no matter what you look like.
490. God wants you to walk then the devil sends a limo.
491. Coffee: Christ offers forgiveness for everyone, everywhere.
492. Bad company ruins good morals.
493. Nothing from nothing leaves nothing.
494. Friends should be like books, few but hand selected.
495. Life is a party so celebrate it.
496. Don't ever let another mother's child cost you your job.
497. Information just seems to go in one ear and out the other.
498. Zebra can't hide his stripes for too long.
499. It's not how you start, it's how you finish.
500. Don't wake up a sleeping giant.

About the Author

Julia (Judy) Buchanan was born in Arkansas, raised in Gary, Indiana, until twelve years old when her family moved back to Chicago, Illinois. She resides in the Chicagoland area with her husband of over fifty years. They have four man-children, four beautiful daughters-in-law, fifteen grandchildren, four grandchildren-in-law, and a host of great-grandchildren. This is her first attempt at writing a book.